CW01212706

The Angel and the Heart of the Storm

Scott M. Stockton

This is a work of fiction.   Names, characters, businesses, places, events, and incidents are either the product of the author's imagination or used in a fictitious manner.   Any resemblance to actual persons, living or dead, is purely coincidental.

Copyright 2017 by Scott M. Stockton
All Rights Reserved

This book is dedicated to the one I love. The man who saved me from my castle tower...and swept me away on journeys I'll never forget.

You gave me life again.

I will always be your treasure.

Part 1

The Angel

Prologue

My name is Tempest. According to my mother, my name means "powerful storm". Though, a hardly feel like a windy tornado, or a watery gale force hurricane. To some, it seems a little silly to name their boy Tempest, but when I was born, that's exactly what was happening outside. A storm. I guess that's why she chose the name. It's never really bothered me, and my friends think it's cool. I seem like any other ordinary teenager in my senior class, but I'm not. I seem to "stand out" a little. I was born with onyx black hair, dark blue eyes, and tanned skin, which I came to learn, was known as the olive complexion. Ever since I was little, my mother has had long hair. She used to let me brush it whenever I wanted. She didn't mind the fact that I wanted long hair too. So, from then on, I let it grow. Now, my hair goes down past my lower back, and I quite often keep it in a nice long braid. I never want to cut it.   School wasn't really hard for me in the early years…until something happened.   And this is my story.

Chapter 1

My Little Secret

Tempest stared down at the paper on his desk.   After realizing he'd forgotten to study the night before he was now facing the fact on how difficult his science test was.   He'd already gotten some of the answers.   Whether they were right or not was another story.   Tempest glanced beside him.   His long time friends, Frances Fry, Willa Hamberg, and Justin Gold all seemed to be doing just fine.   Especially Frances.   She'd always been the logical thinker and brainiac.   Looking through her glasses with her green eyes, she slightly twirled her light brown hair as she answered each question.   Willa was like the exact opposite. Always quick to make decisions, the little red head was busy doodling little pictures of flowers on her test paper since she was finished.   Then there was Justin.   This dark brown haired fellow was busy checking out the girl beside him. He also was finished with his science test and the girl beside him couldn't help but give a snide look and roll her eyes. Her name was Ramona McBee, and she had a reputation of being quite bitchy. Which was one thing her boyfriend, Nathan DuGally, loved about her.

Justin made a sweet gesture, and then laughed quietly as Ramona gave him her middle finger. Justin never really let other people get to him. He actually thought Ramona was feisty and he loved her short black hair with purple highlights. Nathan saw what was happening and he sneered at Justin scornfully. Tempest let out a sigh and he placed a hand over his eyes. The bell suddenly rang and the students in the classroom got up now that class was over. It was now, Tempest realized he'd sat through the entire class period wracking his brain and not even finishing. He swallowed hard and then went to his teacher's desk. Mr. Cass looked up with a look of question.
"Yes, Mr. Thorn?" he asked.
"I didn't finish my test…and…well…I'd like to take it home and bring it back tomorrow" Tempest said quietly. Mr. Cass took his glasses off and let out a sigh.
"You realize this the second time you've done this, Mr. Thorn" he said. "You've got to focus more and study when I tell you to." Tempest hung his head down and his black bangs covered his eyes.
"Sorry" he said timidly. Mr. Cass got up

from his chair and started to erase the white words off the chalk board behind him.

"I can't let you take it home, but you can always come back during your study hall period and finish it then. It's up to you" he said. Tempest raised his head. He was glad his teacher was giving him a break. He knew during his lunch period before study hall, he could study a little and then come back.

"Okay, thanks Mr. Cass. I'll be here then" Tempest said. He left the paper on his teacher's desk and went out the door to meet his friends who were waiting for him.

"How'd you do?" Frances asked, as she pushed her glasses back up to her eyes. Tempest frowned.

"Isn't it obvious?" he asked. "I have to come back during study hall."

"Well, at least he didn't make you start over" Willa said. Justin smiled and walked over beside Tempest and gave him a manly slap on the back.

"Oh, don't worry, Stormy, you'll get it done!" he said with delight. Tempest narrowed his eyes, but then smiled lightly.

"Yeah…thanks" he replied.

Later that day, when Tempest came home, his mother greeted him happily as she came out of the kitchen with an apron around her waist. Her long brown hair was up in messy bun, and Tempest couldn't help but smile.

"Hi, sweetie!" she said.

"Hi, mom" Tempest answered as he flung his back pack down on the living room sofa.

"How was school?" she asked.   Tempest turned on the TV and held the throw pillow that sat beside him.

"Fine, I guess" he said.   Emma Thorn walked over to her son and stood beside him.

"And what about the science test?" she asked.   Tempest gave a nervous look.

"Well…I didn't get it done, but…"

"Tempest, you need to stop daydreaming in class" his mother interrupted.

"I wasn't daydreaming!   I…just forgot to study, but I finished it later on anyway" Tempest said quickly.   Emma shook her head and smiled again.

"You're such a brat" she teased as she ruffled her son's hair and laughed.

"Hey!" Tempest confronted.   He then tossed the small throw pillow at his mother, but she quickly jumped aside and laughed some more. She, like him, was much like a kid at heart. Tempest then found himself laughing while trying to keep a straight face.

"So, what are we having for dinner?" he asked.

"Stuffed shells" Emma said.   "Then after that, we're going to the mall."   Tempest's face smiled with delight.

"Are you going to buy me a present?!" he asked.

"Well yeah, tomorrow's your birthday, silly" Emma said. "You're going to be eighteen!" Tempest then brought that thought to mind. All of his friends were already eighteen, and sometimes he felt he was behind, even though he really wasn't. Emma went back into the kitchen again to set the table.

"Are you going to invite your friends over?" she called out to him. Tempest left his thoughts.

"Yeah, I already said they could come" he responded. "Just remember that Frances is allergic to chocolate."

"I know. I've already gotten a white cake instead" Emma said. Tempest then went back to his thoughts. *"I'm finally going to be eighteen, but I don't really feel any different."*

After walking around the mall to a few stores, Tempest and his mother sat at an ice cream parlor for a break. Emma noticed her son was picking at his ice cream while in thought. So, she decided to bring up a topic she'd been wanting to for a few days.

"So, when are you going to bring home pretty girl for me to meet?" she asked. Tempest snapped his head up with his blue eyes widened.

"Wha...What do ya mean?" he managed to say. Emma shrugged her shoulders.

"I was just curious, that's all" she said. Tempest set his spoon aside and thought to himself again. *"How should I know...I've never really been interested in anyone."*

Tempest suddenly noticed something as he looked up.   A boy came into the ice cream parlor and slowly walked up to the counter to order.   He had short dark brown hair and he seemed to be around Tempest's age, maybe a little older.   He wore a bright colored shirt, light blue to be exact, and jeans with a few holes in the front by the knees.   As he ordered, he pushed his bright red colored handbag up onto his shoulder.   On the bag, in silver letters, it said: *Princess.*

Tempest found himself staring curiously at the other boy's entire physique.   He was just like Tempest.   Quite muscular and thin.   Tempest's eyes followed as the boy got his ice cream and sat down on the other side of the parlor.   Meanwhile, Emma had noticed this and smiled softly to herself.

"Do ya like him?" she asked.   Tempest again gave another look of surprise.   Then he folded his arms and turned his head away from her.

"As if he'd even be interested in me" he said.   He then realized what exactly he'd just said, and turned back to his mother with another look of embarrassment.   His face was completely red. Emma smiled again and took a bite of her ice cream.

"I knew it" she lightly teased.   Tempest's eyes narrowed.

"Knew what?" he asked.   Emma just simply got up from her chair.

"I'll be right back, I'm going to use to

restroom" she said with the smile still on her face. Tempest watched her leave.

"Whatever" he said to himself.

While his mother was gone, Tempest shot a few curious glances over at the other boy.   He in return, looked at him too.   Tempest looked quickly down at his ice cream, but soon found his eyes wandering back over.   The other boy smiled lightly and got up from his chair.   Tempest watched as he came right directly over to him, and sat down at his table.

"You like vanilla too?" he asked.   Tempest was frozen.   Then he looked down at his ice cream bowl.

"Um...yeah" he responded.   The other boy spoke again.

"Not very many people eat just plain vanilla anymore.   But it's always been my favorite" he said.   Tempest blinked.

"Mine too."

The two sat in silence for a moment until the boy spoke again.

"What's your name?" he asked.

"Tempest."

The other boy smiled softly.   His brown eyes twinkled off the hanging lights above them.

"That's a rare name" he said.   Tempest blinked again and nodded.   "Here" the boy said, holding out a piece of paper.   Tempest slowly took it from him.

"See ya" the boy said.   He then got up and

walked out of the parlor.   Tempest looked at the paper and he saw a phone number on it with the name, Malachi, written below it.   Tempest then realized his mother was standing beside him looking at the paper too.   He looked at her and blushed again, and she just smiled.

Chapter 2

A Walk In the Park

Tempest and his mother arrived home later the same day. Emma hadn't mentioned anything about what had happened at the mall. She simply acted in her usual way. She sat on the couch crocheting something in light pink yarn as she watched *Roseanne* on TV, laughing now and then at Roseanne's outgoing remarks. Tempest sat on the other end of the couch. He secretly held the little paper with the number on it in his hands.

"Are you going to call him?" his mother said at last. Tempest looked over at her, and tried to find the courage to speak. He swallowed hard and pushed out some words.

"Do...do you still care about me, mom?" he

asked.   Emma stopped her crochet needles.

"Of course, Tempest.   I love you very much.   I've known for a while now.   The question is, how do *you* feel about it?" she answered.   Tempest sat there in thought.   He'd always realized he hadn't been attracted to females, but he noticed at times a few of the other guys at school without even making an effort.

"I...don't know" he said.   Emma turned off the TV and set her project on the coffee table.   She leaned over to her son and spoke softly.

"I still love you" she said again.   "You be whoever you want to be.   I'll always be proud of you."

With that said, Tempest made a small smile.

"Thanks, mom" he said.   Emma smiled back and kissed his forehead.   She then got up and walked toward the stairs.

"I'm a bit tired, so I'm going up to bed. Goodnight" she said.

"Goodnight" Tempest returned.

Emma went upstairs and Tempest looked at the little paper again.   He got up and went upstairs to his own room, closing the door behind him.   He sat the paper on his computer desk and glanced at his wall clock.   "It's only nine o'clock, he should still be awake" he said to himself.   Tempest reached for his phone and dialed the number on the paper.   He felt a wave of nervous tension rise inside him as he heard someone answer.   It was a woman's voice asking hello.

"Um...is Malachi there?" he asked timidly.

"Just a moment" the woman said.
Tempest waited as the phone was handed over.

"Hello?" Malachi asked.

"Hi...this is Tempest."

"Oh, hey there, I was wondering when you'd call" Malachi said.   Tempest sat in silence and began to fiddle with the end of his long hair braid.

"So...what'd you want to talk about?" he asked.   Realizing Tempest was nervous, Malachi kept it casual.

"Nothing much, you just looked a little lonely sitting by yourself at the ice cream place" he said.

"I wasn't really alone.   My mom was in the restroom" Tempest said.

"Oh, you mean the woman that sat across from you?" Malachi asked.

"Yeah"

"She cares for you a lot.   I'll bet when your father left, she was devastated, but she's happy you're with her" Malachi acknowledged.
Tempest dropped his braid in surprise.

"How'd you...know?" he asked.

"I pick up on things" Malachi confessed.
Tempest smiled to himself.   Malachi was right and Tempest had never really told anyone about that, except for his friends.

"So, where do you live?" Malachi questioned.

"Huh?"

"What street do you live on?"

"Oh...Clayton Avenue" Tempest answered.

"Good, you're nearby. Can you meet me at the park tomorrow afternoon?" Malachi asked.

"Well...tomorrow's my birthday, but the party doesn't start until later, so...yeah I can" Tempest said.

"Really? Good, it's a date then. See ya tomorrow around twelve" Malachi said. Tempest blushed and responded timidly.

"Okay...bye" he said.

"Bye" Malachi returned. Then they both hung up. Tempest felt a new feeling creep through him. Was he excited? He couldn't really tell. All he knew was, he liked it.

The next day was Saturday. Tempest hadn't told his mother yet that he'd called Malachi. So, when the grandfather clock in the living room sounded its chimes for eleven thirty, Tempest realized he had to tell her he was going to the park.

"Aw, I'm glad you called him" Emma teased with a sweet tone. Tempest shot a glare while being embarrassed. Then he sighed and spoke.

"I'll be back before my friends get here later" he said.

"Okay, have fun!" his mother called as he went out the door.

It was a nice sunny spring day as Tempest walked the four blocks to the small park down the avenue. He soon realized that Malachi must live nearby too, for when he got to the park, he saw the other boy standing against a light post, waiting for him. He had a small digital camera with a strap hanging around his neck, and he held the same red handbag as before on his shoulder. He wore another bright colored shirt, this time a light purple, and he turned his head and smiled as Tempest approached him.

"Hey there" he said openly.

"Hi" Tempest said simply. Malachi turned his eyes to the little brick path beside him.

"Shall we?"

Tempest nodded in reply.

The two of them walked slowly, side by side, as a light zephyr blew and the birds chirped in the trees above.

"What's the camera for?" Tempest asked.

"Well...I like to take pictures of things. Nature, art, and random things that I might feel are rare" Malachi said. Tempest smiled a little to the fact that he thought Malachi was different. He'd never met anyone like him before, and that same new feeling was coming back again.

"I see you" Malachi said.

"See...me?" Tempest asked.

"See you smiling" Malachi answered. Tempest blushed and turned his head away slightly. Malachi thought it was cute.

"I like your braid. It must have taken some time to grow it" he said. Tempest looked at the boy again.

"Thanks...I've never cut it before" he responded quietly.

"You don't have to be so nervous, I realize this is new for you" Malachi said.

"Really?" Tempest asked widening his eyes.
"Yeah, and it's okay with me" Malachi said. Tempest smiled again and reassured himself that he was okay. The two boys came up to a large willow tree with its long branches hanging low to the ground. Malachi stopped as he looked at the elegant tree, and he softly took Tempest by the hand.

"Come on, let's sit under the tree" he said. Tempest blushed some more and followed his new friend without being reluctant.

They sat down on the soft grass, beside each other, looking up into the tree.

"Willows are so magical" Malachi said aloud.

"Yeah, they aren't like any other tree. Their...unique" Tempest said. Feeling the same way, Malachi looked at Tempest in amazement.

"So, how old are you today?" he asked.

"Eighteen" Tempest said. "What about you?"

"I'm twenty" Malachi answered. Tempest had already assumed Malachi was around that age, and it didn't bother him. Suddenly Malachi noticed a monarch butterfly fly by and land on a small flower in front of them.

"Look" he said softly. Tempest saw the butterfly too. He thought it was beautiful in color.

"It's so...pretty" he said with wide eyes. Malachi began to raise his camera up to take a picture, when another monarch butterfly landed on the same flower.

"Two of them" he said in surprise. Tempest smiled.

"They must be together" he said. Malachi snapped the picture and it showed up on the digital screen as the butterflies flew away. Malachi smiled again too, and he scooted up against Tempest.

"Let's get a picture of ourselves" he said.

"Um...okay" Tempest said shyly. They leaned close to each other and smiled as Malachi snapped another picture. At this moment, the feeling inside Tempest was getting stronger. Malachi felt it too. They began to look into each other's eyes, adoring their colors. And that's when it happened. Malachi leaned in and pressed his lips against Tempest's. Startled at first with the new experience, Tempest tensed up. Then slowly, he fell into it, and returned the kiss. It felt so good and right to him, and he breathed in the smell of Malachi's wonderful cologne. After pulling back, Malachi smiled at Tempest and spoke.

"That was your first one...wasn't it?" Tempest nodded.

"Yeah" he said, blushing even more. Malachi looked down at the camera and then showed Tempest the picture of them together under the willow tree.

"I'll give you a copy once I print them out" he said.

"Okay" Tempest said.

Holding hands as they walked out of the park, it now came time for them to separate and go back home. By this time, Tempest and Malachi had already given each other their addresses.

"I'll call you later, after you've had your birthday party" Malachi said.

"You can come over if you want" Tempest said, hoping he'd say yes.

"I'd like to, but I'm going out to dinner with my parents. So I won't be able to come" Malachi said. Tempest hung his head and Malachi put a hand under his chin.

"Don't worry, we can do something again tomorrow okay?" he said. Tempest raised his head and smiled lightly.

"Okay."

Chapter 3

True Friends

Tempest walked through the front door casually, and his mother came over to him. She noticed he was smiling and blushing at the same time.

"Did you kiss him?" she asked eagerly. Tempest didn't speak, but nodded in reply. Emma clapped her hands together with delight.

"Aw, how sweet!" she said. Tempest then hung his head down and frowned. "What's the matter, dear?" his mother asked. This thought had been bothering Tempest as he had walked home, and he didn't know what to do about it. "Tempest...what's wrong?" Emma asked again with concern.

"I have to tell my friends" Tempest said

quietly. Emma put her arms around her son and hugged him.

"Don't worry, I'll help you" she said softly.

"But…what if…they don't accept me" Tempest said, his eyes welling with tears. Emma brought her son's head up and looked into his eyes.

"Then they're not you're true friends" she said.

The party had come all too quick for Tempest. One by one his friends arrived saying happy birthday to him, and giving him gifts. Putting on a happy front, he smiled and acted natural. However, Frances saw right through it. Willa and Justin didn't, and so, when Tempest was alone in the kitchen, Frances made an effort to find out why her friend was different.

"Did something happen today?" she asked. Tempest froze.

"What do mean?" he asked cautiously, not even looking directly at her.

"Oh come on, it's obvious, at least for me anyway" she said. Tempest turned around and barely spoke above a whisper.

"I've…met someone" he said. Frances looked confused.

"Who?" she asked. Tensing up again, Tempest shook his head.

"Never mind, it's not important" he said. Frances raised an eyebrow and narrowed her eyes.

"Yes it is, I can tell, so spill it" she

demanded.   Tempest sighed heavily and realized he had to speak or Frances would never let up.

"A guy" he said.

"A guy?   What guy?" Frances asked in confusion.

"He's a little older than me, well...twenty to be exact and I met him at the mall yesterday" Tempest said.

"So" Frances said flatly.

"So...today we went to the park and..."

"And what?"

"We...kissed."

Frances stood there, silent for a moment, as Tempest had his eyes closed in embarrassment and fear.   She smiled and put a hand on his shoulder.

"I always knew" she said.   Tempest opened his eyes quickly and looked at his friend in shock.

"You...did?"
Frances laughed.

"Well duh, it's obvious.   You've never had a girlfriend and whenever a girl hits on you, you back away in disgust" Frances said.

"So" Tempest said.

"*So*...I don't care if you're gay.   That's one of the things I like about you.   I'm just glad you finally told me" she said with a smile.   Tempest stood there in shock.   Not only did this surprise him, but he was also happy she accepted him.

"Can you...help me tell the others?" he asked.

"Sure. Just remember, take your time if you're not ready yet" she said.

"I...think I am" he said.

"Okay then, let's go" Frances said, pulling on Tempest's wrist.

Frances lead Tempest into the living room where Willa and Justin sat.

"There you are, Stormy, I thought you'd never bring my drink to me" Justin announced. Tempest sat on the couch beside his mother and Willa. Justin sat across in a chair, and Frances stood.

"You guys, Tempest has something to tell you" Frances said. Emma looked surprised at the fact that her son had told his friend, and was now going to tell the others.

"What?" Justin asked.

Tempest was scared again; he closed his eyes and decided to say it.

"You guys...I'm gay!" he blurted out. Like Frances once was, Willa and Justin were both speechless for the moment. Then Willa's eyes lit up.

"Really? Wow! Now we can go shopping together!" she said happily. Emma burst out laughing, and Tempest opened his eyes.

"He even has a boyfriend" Frances added, and Tempest shot a glare.

"Oh! Who is it?! You've got to tell me!" Willa said. Tempest didn't respond. He was too worried about what Justin thought. Justin looked at Tempest in puzzlement.

"I always had my suspicions, but..."

"I've never felt that way about *you*, Justin!" Tempest said quickly.   Slowly, Justin formed a smile.

"Oh well, you'll always be the same to me, Stormy!" he said as he gave Tempest another manly slap on the back.   Tempest was now feeling better.   No longer did he have a sickly feeling in his stomach.   His friends...were truly his friends, and he was glad to have them with him.

"Just please don't tell anyone else at school about this" he said.

"Don't worry, if you're not ready, we'll keep quiet" Frances said.

"Thanks you guys" Tempest said quietly.

"So...what's he like?" Willa asked eagerly. Tempest blushed at the thought.

"Um..."

Emma laughed again.

"He's a real cutie, right Tempest?" his mother teased.   Tempest folded his arms, trying to be serious, and he nodded slowly.

"When can we meet him?" Willa asked.

"Willa, you're embarrassing him" Frances confronted.

"Oh, I was just curious!" Willa said. Tempest sighed heavily again.

After his friends left for the night, Tempest laid on his bed, thinking about what had happened with Malachi. A few times, he wondered if he'd dreamed it. Although he knew it had been very real. He felt content with it, and happy to have experienced it. He remembered the way Malachi had kissed him, and putting a hand on his lips, he realized...he'd never forget it.

Suddenly the phone rang, and Tempest jumped up from his bed to answer it. He quickly said hello as he knew who it was.
"Hey" Malachi said. "How was your party?"
"Good. I...told my friends" Tempest said. Realizing what Tempest meant, Malachi smiled.
"I'm glad you did" he said.
"Really?"
"Yeah, you shouldn't be afraid to be yourself."
Tempest felt a wave of happiness come over him. *"He's glad I told them"* he thought to himself.
"It was a little scary" he said.
"I'm sure it was. I felt the same way when I first came out" Malachi said.
"How did your parents take it?" Tempest asked.
"They told me they already knew" Malachi answered. Tempest chuckled.
"That's what *my* mom said"
Malachi couldn't help but laugh too. He thought Tempest was so cute when he was shy.
"I like your laugh" he said. Tempest was nervous again, but he felt excited too.

"And I like...the way your voice is" he said.

"Well, thank you" Malachi said happily. "Anyway, how'd you like to go to the mall with me tomorrow?"

"Yeah, I'd like too, but... I'll have to see if my mom can take me there" Tempest said.

"Don't worry about it.   I'll come and get you" Malachi proposed.

"You will?"

"Yeah, be ready by noon again, and I'll see you then" Malachi said.

"Okay."

"Bye for now."

"Bye."

After hanging up his phone, Tempest smiled and lay back down on his bed.   He stared up at the ceiling, thinking about Malachi of course. Things seemed to be changing so quickly, and Tempest felt good about himself.

Chapter 4

At the Mall

    Tempest eagerly waited for the clock to chime noon.　He told his mom he didn't know how long he'd be gone, but she told him she didn't mind and to have fun.　As if the doorbell had been attached to the clock, it suddenly rang as the clock chimed.　Tempest opened the door and Malachi stood there with flowers in his hand.　Tempest thought he was about to melt as he took the tiger lilies from Malachi.　Emma came up behind and saw the little present.

    "This must be the famous Malachi Harper" she said.　Tempest sniffed his flowers and then handed them to Emma.

    "They're from my mom's garden" Malachi said proudly.

    "Well, I'll be sure to put them in a very

lovely vase" Emma said.   Blushing deep red, Tempest smiled lightly as Malachi took him by the hand.

They walked up to a very eye-catching light blue convertible as Malachi opened the passenger door.   Tempest gazed at the classic 1957 Ford Thunderbird in complete surprise.   It appeared to be in mint condition, which is rare for a car of its age.   Wide white-walls decorated the tires, and the sun beamed across the car like a shimmering wind from a dream.   Tempest began to feel like he was in a movie scene.

"I...*really* like your car" he said with a wide smile.

"Wait 'till ya ride in it" Malachi said.   "It was my grandpa's car when he was younger.   He left it to me after he passed away."

Tempest's mother was standing on the porch behind them with her arms folded, and leaning against the doorframe.   She had a calmed smile on her face, and Tempest knew she already approved of this new boy in his life.

"You're very lucky, Malachi"   she commented in delight.   "That car is gorgeous!" Malachi returned a smile and thanked the woman as he seated Tempest in the car.

Riding down the highway, Tempest and Malachi enjoyed the wind through their hair. Tempest's long black braid trailed behind him like a snake, and Malachi liked it.   He also couldn't help but gaze at Tempest's nicely tanned, and very strong arms since Tempest had chosen to wear a tank top with his jeans.   Malachi had the radio playing loud, as the song "Stupid Cupid" by Connie Francis swept along the wind.   It reminded Tempest of a movie scene, and he liked the way Malachi sang along with Connie.   Having no shame that he couldn't quite match the singer's iconic voice.   It made him smile as he watched him sing, and Malachi knew this.   He occasionally grinned at Tempest and gave a wink as the rock n' roll melody lured him into singing along.   Soon, both boys were shaking their hips to the beat, and Tempest felt a sense of freedom come over him. Like the sudden thought of flying without wings, high above the earth without a care in the world. This boy was bringing something new and exciting to his life, and he was loving every minute of it.

    They strolled together around the mall, looking at many different things and allowing their relationship to grow.   They bought milkshakes at the ice cream parlor, and looked at the pictures from the day before.   Tempest and Malachi proudly placed smaller versions of the picture they had of themselves in their wallets.   While Tempest casually waited by a store's entrance, Malachi secretly bought his new boyfriend a birthday present.   Tempest saw Malachi finally come back, and he was holding something behind him.
    "I bought you something" he said.
    "What is it?" Tempest blinked.   Malachi

revealed the gift and Tempest's dark blue eyes lit up. In Malachi's hand, was a little stuffed penguin with a red ribbon around its neck. Absolutely delighted that Malachi remembered that penguins were one of his favorite animals, Tempest chose this moment to kiss his boyfriend with strong emotion. Nearby, without them knowing, Ramona McBee and Nathan DuGally watched with appalling looks.

"Oh my god!" Ramona said with a laugh.
"That's sick!" Nathan exclaimed.

When Tempest pulled back, Malachi smiled at him with his brown eyes seeming to sparkle. Then, Tempest realized something. All around them, people were giving terrible looks to *"the sickos"* and a few mothers shielded their children's eyes. Tempest hung his head low with his bangs covering his sad eyes. Malachi noticed this and he couldn't help but feel his own tears forming.

"It's okay, Tempest, we'll just try to ignore them" he said softly. Tempest couldn't speak. The only thing he could do was cry and clutch Malachi's hands. He only wanted to kiss him. Why was that so bad?

"Let's go to my house. I'd like you to meet my parents" Malachi suggested. Tempest raised his head.

"Okay" he said weakly.

Chapter 5

Ponytails

By the time Malachi arrived at his home, Tempest had dried his tears. Malachi turned off the engine and lightly held Tempest's hand. Tempest looked at him with a frown, and Malachi gently brushed his black bangs from his boyfriend's eyes.

"I think you'll like them" he said. They both got out of the car and walked up to the front door. To their surprise, it opened and a woman stood there.

"Hi, mom. This is Tempest Thorn, the guy I was telling you about" Malachi said. Mrs. Harper greeted Tempest with a warm smile.

"Welcome to our home. I'm Mary" she said.

"Hello" said Tempest.

Mary walked the two boys into the living room where Malachi's father sat on the couch.

"This is my dad" Malachi said. The man stood up and shook hands with Tempest.

"Hello there, young sir. My name's Gordon" he said with a deep voice. "Malachi talks about you a lot around here."

"Oh really?" Tempest asked with a blush.

"Well, Tempest, I hope you like eggplant parmesan" Mary said.

"Yeah, very much" Tempest said. He was already feeling much more comfortable.

"I'll show you to the dining room" Gordon said, as he led Tempest there.

"You've really found someone special, Malachi. He's very handsome" Mary said. Malachi smiled and thanked his mother.

The dinner had proved to be welcoming to Tempest. Malachi's family was very polite. Tempest knew that in today's world, it was sometimes hard to find people like them. After dinner was over, Tempest realized Malachi was in the small downstairs bathroom, combing his hair at the mirror. Curious about it, Tempest walked in to see him.

"Oh...hi there Tempest" Malachi said.

"What are you doing?" Tempest asked.

"Just combing my hair" Malachi answered.

"Oh. I thought it looked good the way it was" Tempest admitted.

"Really?" Malachi asked. He was

surprised. Nobody had ever commented his hair before.

"Yeah" Tempest said with a small blush. Malachi set down his comb. He looked at Tempest and made a small smile.

"You're cute when you blush like that" he said softly. Tempest looked up at Malachi with big eyes.

"You…really think so?" he asked. Malachi simply nodded and took Tempest by the hand. He slowly brought him over in front of the mirror.

"What are doing now?" Tempest asked.

"Just relax" Malachi said quietly.

Tempest watched in the mirror as his boyfriend slowly undid his long braid. Malachi began to run his comb through Tempest's long and beautiful black hair.

"Your hair is very soft. You take care of it well" said Malachi with a gentle tone. Tempest soon found himself liking the feel of Malachi fingers in his hair and he closed his eyes.

"Thanks" he said. Malachi opened a drawer beside him and pulled out two hair ties. After parting Tempest's hair, he gradually made two ponytails, one on each side of Tempest's head, behind his ears. He then came close to one of Tempest's ears and softly told him to open his eyes. When Tempest did this, he saw his new ponytails and instantly liked them. He smiled and looked at Malachi. During this moment, Malachi stole a kiss. Tempest put his arms around Malachi's waist, and pulled him close.

After the kiss, Tempest rested his head upon Malachi's shoulder.

"I hope…what we're doing…is natural. I've never done this before…but I've always wanted to" Tempest confessed.

"I know" said Malachi.   "Just take your time."

"This *has* to be right, otherwise I wouldn't feel this way…about you" Tempest whispered.

"I'm glad you do.   And don't worry…its right if you want it to be."

Chapter 6

Absence

    For the next few weeks, Tempest and Malachi often went on dates.   They would go around to town, doing random things on the spur of the moment, just talking about their past or what they liked.   Every time Tempest went out with him, he felt different.   Alive inside, and so content.   Malachi was so outgoing and caring, and Tempest found himself liking him even more.   His insides would do flip-flops, and he knew something about this was special.   Even though it was all becoming gradually natural, Tempest still felt nervous.   Although, it was okay, because…Malachi didn't rush him.   He let Tempest find himself on his own accord.   He just gently gave him a little push forward every now and then...and Tempest realized he was letting him.

The next morning, Tempest woke up in his bed and realized he'd slept all night with his ponytails. The night before, he had decided not to ruin them, by taking out the hair ties. Although, since Tempest tossed and turned in his sleep sometimes, he saw the hair ties were ready to come out.

After taking a shower and getting dressed for school, he suddenly heard the phone ring. He picked up the receiver and realized it was Malachi.

"Hi" a soft voice said.

"Hi, Malachi. What are you calling so early for?" Tempest asked with a yawn.

"I have to tell you something" Malachi said sadly. Noticing the change in his voice, Tempest knew something was wrong.

"What's the matter?" he asked.

"My grandmother's sick. My family and I have to go to the hospital and see her" Malachi said.

"Do you want me to meet you there?" Tempest asked.

"You...can't"

"Why?"

"She lives in California. We're going there to see her."

Tempest felt himself tense up.

"For...how long?" he asked cautiously.

"I don't know" Malachi answered. "It might be permanent...I'm sorry."

Tempest didn't know what to say.   He simply stood there and realized Malachi was going to be well over a thousand miles away from where they lived.

"Are you okay?" Malachi asked nervously. Tempest could hardly make words.

"Yeah…um…please…come back" he said softly through his tears.

"I'll come back…I promise" Malachi said. Tempest fought hard to hold back his tears.   "I have to go now; we have to catch a plane at the airport.   I'll call you when I get there…be strong" Malachi said.

"Wait!   Malachi…I…love you!" Tempest said aloud.   However, Malachi didn't hear him, since he had already hung up the phone. Tempest heard the dial tone and he dropped the receiver to the floor.   He knew now, what the feeling had grown to be.   He felt his tears flow down his face.   His mother slowly walked up to him and put her hand on his shoulder.   *"Come back!"* he yelled in his mind. *"Please…"*   He turned around and embraced his mother, who by that time had already been crying herself.

Tempest didn't go to school that day.   Nor the next.   He didn't want to go anywhere.   By the time his friends had come to visit, he'd be in his room…alone.   His hair…done up in ponytails. Laying on his bed…and staring at the picture…while holding his penguin.   Frances, Willa, and Justin came into his room and stood beside him.   Since Emma had told them what had happened, they already felt the need to comfort him.

"Hi, Tempest" Willa said quietly.

"Hi" he said in the same way.

"Don't worry...he'll come back.   He said he would" Frances said.   Tempest gave a small laugh of hopelessness.

"No Frances...he won't."

"Sure he will.   Do you honestly think a boy that cute could ever stay away from you?" Willa asked.   Tempest looked at his friend.

"But...what if he doesn't?"   he asked her. And for the first time, Willa felt speechless.   Not even Justin knew what to say.   Frances knelt down beside her friend, and looked into his eyes.

"He'll be back.   Absence makes the heart grow stronger.   He can't stay away from you forever" she said.   Tempest, for the first time in several hours, made a small smile.

"I hope so, Frances.   I think I...love him."

Several miles away, in San Francisco, Malachi and his parents entered the room in the hospital where his grandmother was staying. The elderly woman on the white bed looked up at her grandson slowly.

"Hello, dear" she said.

"Hi, Grandma Helen" Malachi said.   "How are you feeling?"

"Oh...a little under the weather" she said with a cough.   Malachi sat down on a chair beside her.

"Hello Gordon" Helen said.

"Hi, mom.   Did the doctors say whether or not the medicine will work?" Gordon asked anxiously.

"They'll know by morning" Helen said. "If you'll excuse us, my grandson has something to tell me."   Gordon and Mary nodded and left the room, closing the door behind them.   Malachi looked at his grandmother.

"How'd you know?" he asked.   Helen smiled.

"I pick up on things.   You got it from me" she said.   Malachi was surprised.   "So...tell me about this boy of yours" she said.   Malachi smiled with a blush.

"He's very special" he said.

"Is he now?" Helen asked.   Malachi nodded.   Helen put her hand on Malachi's arm slowly.

"Can I see a picture of him?" she asked weakly.   Malachi took out his wallet from his red bag, and removed the picture.   Helen looked at it with her elderly brown eyes.

"Oh...he is so handsome, Malachi" she said slowly, but happily.   "You should feel very proud to be with him."

"I do, Grandma.   He...means the world to me" Malachi said in tears.

"You should go back to him...he needs you" Helen said weakly.

"I know, Grandma" Malachi said sadly.   He feared his grandmother's death so much, and now it seemed like he couldn't stop it.

"Just remember, Malachi, he's very

sensitive. He needs your love" Helen said.
"Grandma...I..."
"You love him..."
"Yes"
"And he loves you...more than you know"

Malachi couldn't stop his tears, as he watched his grandmother pass away on the bed. He thought about what she'd said, and knew she right.

"I'm going to tell him, Grandma..."

Tempest heard his phone and he jumped up from his bed. He was so happy to hear Malachi's voice; he began to cry on the phone. Malachi told him about his grandmother. About what she had said, and about her death. Tempest felt so bad for him, and he told him to take his time coming back home. However, Malachi insisted on coming back after his grandmother's funeral. So, Tempest said he'd be waiting for him at the airport when he arrives. Malachi said it would be a couple of days, and not to worry, he was definitely coming back to him.

Chapter 7

Life As We Know It

Tempest went to school the next day, feeling better. His hair was back into it's nice long braid and he greeted his friends as they sat down in their desks beside him.

"Hi, Tempest" Frances said.

"Are you feeling better now?" Willa asked.

"Yeah. He's coming back tomorrow" Tempest said with a smile. Justin noticed the picture Tempest was holding, and he sat down in front of him.

"Can I see what he looks like?" he asked. Tempest, a little surprised, handed over his picture for Justin to see.

"He looks like he's a nice guy" Justin said, and he gave back the picture.

"Thanks" Tempest said.   Without him knowing, another boy stood behind him silently.

"Hi, Shayler" Willa said to the boy.

Shayler Bird, another student in the class, was often quiet and serious.   He looked down at Tempest's picture with interest.   Tempest had noticed this, and was wondering what he could be thinking.

"Um…Shayler?" he asked.

"Your boyfriend is very lucky" Shayler said. Tempest was confused.

"Huh?"

"He's lucky because…he has you" Shayler said.   At that moment, Tempest was blushing at the fact that Shayler had always liked him more than just a friend.   Shayler smiled and he returned to his seat.

"Wow" Willa said quietly.   Frances and Justin were just as shocked.

"Um…thanks, Shayler" Tempest said.

After class was over, Tempest walked down the hallway to his locker with his friends.   He was excited at the fact that Malachi was coming home the next day, and he couldn't help but think about it.

"You know, Tempest, we still have to meet this boyfriend of yours" Willa said.

"Yeah, I'll bet he's just as cute in person, as he is in the picture" Frances teased.   Tempest laughed and he turned his attention to his locker. His face suddenly became confused. There, sticking out of the locker door was a folded piece of paper. He friends noticed it to. Tempest pulled it out and opened it up casually. There was a sudden crash as Tempest dropped his text book to the floor. The echo surprised his friends in the empty hall. His head hung low and his bangs hid his eyes.

"Tempest?" Willa asked with caution. Tempest dropped the paper and with one strong punch, he hit the locker door, leavening and ugly dent in the metal

"Fuck!" he exclaimed. His friends stared at him with concerned expressions. Frances picked up the paper and saw what was on it. In the middle was a hideous picture of two stick figures in a sexual position. Below it, in capital letters, was the word "faggot" sprawled across it with bright red ink for attention.

Willa gasped at the paper, and Frances noticed the tears running down Tempest's face. He stood there, motionless, and the words he spoke came out shaky and saddened.

"Why? Why does the world have to hate...people like me?" he managed to say. Willa began to feel her own tears as well. Frances crumbled up the paper and dropped it to the floor, without looking away from her friend.

"People...are cruel" she said softly. "They fear what is different or what they don't understand, and they only get lost in their own stupidity." Tempest brought his hands up to face while crying and Frances put her arms around him.

"Not me. I don't feel that way about you" Justin spoke up. Tempest raised his head, his eyes were very melancholy.

"We'll always be here for you" Willa said.

"Come on...let's get you home" Frances whispered.

Chapter 8

Distant Thoughts

As Tempest lay on his bed and looked at his little stuffed penguin, he couldn't help but think about Malachi. Now that others at school knew about him being gay, he was afraid to go back. It was late at night now, and he knew his mother was probably sleeping. Before Tempest met Malachi, his life was missing something. He knew now what it was. Tempest's heart was longing for Malachi's touch.

Miles up in the air, Malachi looked out his airplane window at the night sky. The clouds looked as if they were slowly dancing around, with the moon shining incandescently through them.

He had been riding for what it seemed like for days. He sighed and opened his red handbag and took out the picture of him and Tempest. As if by some kind of magic, Tempest and Malachi were looking at the same photograph, and at the same time. Malachi stroked in fingers slowly over Tempest's smile. He felt something inside him. He felt pain. Emotional pain. The same pain that Tempest was feeling too. There was a connection between them. It couldn't really be explained, and it didn't have to be. They could feel each other's presence...each other's spirit across time.
"Please...come back to me."
"I'll be back...I promise."

Beside Malachi, a young woman noticed the picture he was holding. She could see how happy they were while together. She then realized Malachi's sullen expression.
"Is that your boyfriend?" she asked quietly. Bringing his attention to the woman, he answered her question after a moment of thought.
"Yeah" he replied. The woman smiled a little.
"He's a cutie...you're very fortunate" she said. Then Malachi smiled back, glad she was one of those rare, kind people.
"Thank you."

The woman then opened a magazine and began to read, leaving Malachi with his private thoughts. Malachi looked back at the picture.

Seeing Tempest's smile, he thought to himself: *"One of the best things about you is your smile.   I'll never let anyone make you frown.   You deserve joy."*

    Emma knocked on Tempest's bedroom door lightly, and she heard her son walk over across the hardwood floor, before opening his door sluggishly.
    "Hi.   Are you okay?" she asked.   Tempest didn't speak as he simply turned around and sat back on his bed.   He left the door open, allowing his mother to enter.   Picking up his little penguin off the bed, Emma sat down beside him.   Tempest stared at the wood grain in the floor, not really wanting to look up.   Emma gently wiped the tears from his eyes with her hand.
    "I just want you to know…I'm very proud of you" she said.   "It takes a lot of courage to stand up to negativity, and you did the best you could."
    "I love him, mom" Tempest spoke up. "I've finally realized that.   I'm sorry I couldn't tell you about myself sooner."
    "You told me when you were ready to…you don't have to be sorry for waiting.   And just think…tomorrow you'll see him again, and you can plant a great big kiss on his face" she said. Tempest looked up and made a small grin at the comment.   "You've made the right choice."

Chapter 9

Being Myself

    Tempest waited anxiously for Malachi to get off the plane.　His flight had been delayed, which didn't make things easier for either of them. However, he promised himself he was going to be strong, and not worry about what others thought. As he watched each passenger came out the door, Tempest began to wrap his long braid around his fingers.　Emma sat quietly on a nearby bench, reading a novel and sipping her coffee.　As Malachi finally emerged on the scene, Tempest dropped his braid.　Malachi saw him and he came over with his bag, a gleeful smile upon his face.
    "I see you've been playing with your hair

again, silly boy" he said.   Tempest stood there in front of him, and spoke just above a whisper.

"You're...back."

"Of course.   After all...I promised you I would be" Malachi said.   Tempest felt his emotion rise and he ran into an embrace.   He was back now.   Nothing else mattered to him except for this moment.

"I missed you" he said through tears. Malachi dropped his bag and raised Tempest's head up to look into his eyes.   He knew he was crying now because of joy, and he gave him such a tender kiss...that Tempest never wanted to let go.

The next day, Tempest built up the courage to go back to school.   He even wore his hair in Malachi's ponytails.   Willa absolutely loved them, and she playfully twisted them with her fingers when she saw them.

"Hey!   You *are* pulling my hair you know!" Tempest said as he backed away.

"Sorry!   You just look so adorable!" Willa teased.   Tempest tried to make a serious face. Shayler noticed Tempest as well.

"Yeah...too bad he's already taken" he spoke up.   Blushing, Tempest folded his arms with a straight face.

"Shayler!   Do you have to be so...blunt?!" he exclaimed.   Shayler simply giggled to himself.

"Okay class, get to your seats.   Our session has already started" Mr. Cass called out.

After class, when the bell rang, Tempest

gathered up books and began to leave the classroom.   He was soon stopped by his teacher on the way to the door.

"I was wondering if might have a word with you, Mr. Thorn?" the teacher asked.

"I'll meet you guys in a minute" Tempest said to his friends.   Frances, Willa and Justin went out in the hall to wait.   Mr. Cass, normally known as a very stern science teacher, removed his glasses from his eyes.

"Mr. Thorn..." he said.   "...I can't imagine how hard it must have been when you found that paper at your locker."   Tempest looked at the man in surprise, then he hung his head in embarrassment.

"You...have no idea" he said.   Mr. Cass looked at his student with a concerned expression.

"I just want you to know, if someone bothers you again, come and tell me.   I'll take care of it" he said.   Tempest raised his head, revealing his eyes.

"I take care for all of my students, Tempest...that includes you too" Mr. Cass said with a smile.   Tempest felt pleased, now that he knew his teacher was on his side.

"Thanks, Mr. Cass" he said.

As he walked with his friends out of the high school, Tempest suddenly saw Malachi standing beside his light blue Thunderbird convertible, waiting for him.

"Aw...he came to get you" Willa said in a girly voice.

"You'd better go to him" Frances said.

"Yeah, he's been waiting there for a while" Justin added. Tempest smiled, and as he approached him, Malachi opened the passenger door.

"Sorry if you waited so long...I didn't know you were out here" Tempest said.

"That's okay, it was worth the wait" Malachi said. Willa and Frances giggled amongst themselves, and Tempest eagerly got into the car.

"So...where are we going?" Tempest asked.

"To my house" Malachi said simply.

Chapter 10

Alone

As Malachi drove into his driveway, Tempest realized his parent's car wasn't there. He got out of the car and walked with Malachi into the house.

"Where's your parents?" he asked.

"They're out for a few days" Malachi said.

"So...it's just...you and me then" Tempest said.

"Just us" Malachi responded.

The two of them walked into the living room, and Tempest sat down on the couch. Malachi looked at the mail on the coffee table and

then put it back.
"Do you want anything to eat or drink?" he asked.
"Not really" Tempest answered.   Malachi then sat down beside him.   After wrapping his arms around him gently, Tempest leaned closer to Malachi and rested his head against his chest, closing his eyes.
"I've been thinking a lot lately.   I know I'm your first boyfriend, Tempest, and...*well*...I'd like to yours forever" Malachi said.   Tempest looked up at Malachi with a smile.
"Really?" he asked.   Malachi nodded, and Tempest felt a wave of joy throughout his entire body.
"Come on...let's go upstairs" Malachi said, getting up.   Tempest felt himself blushing again as he let Malachi lead him to his room.

Malachi's room was truly extraordinary to Tempest.   On the walls, hung many pictures that Malachi had taken with his digital camera.   There were pictures of flowers, animals, decorative buildings, and even one of a marble water fountain.
"These are amazing!" Tempest admired.   Malachi smiled and he handed Tempest a gold picture frame.   In it, were the two monarch butterflies they had seen on their first date.   Tempest held it in appreciation.
"For me?" he asked.   Malachi nodded.
"It was the first time we kissed, Tempest" he said.   "I want you to have the picture...so you

can always remember that." Tempest was truly touched. He set the picture down on the desk beside him and embraced Malachi. He wanted to be with him forever as well.

"I love you, Tempest. You mean everything to me" Malachi said softly. Tempest pulled back and began to blush.

"Can you…prove it to me?" he asked nervously. Malachi held Tempest's hands.

"Are you sure?" he asked. Tempest bit his lip, and then nodded.

Malachi laid his boyfriend down on his bed.

"I've…never done this before" Tempest confessed.

"I know…just relax" Malachi assured him. Tempest then closed his eyes as he felt Malachi's hands reach slowly up his shirt. He felt tense, but Malachi was gentle and un-forceful. Tempest put his arms around Malachi. Thinking this was an okay "sign", Malachi kissed him as he began to unzip his pants. Tempest then began to shake.

"Malachi…s-stop" he said uneasily. Malachi opened his eyes.

"What's wrong" he asked quietly.

"I…can't. Please…just stop" Tempest said. Malachi let up and sat down on the bed beside him.

"You're not ready" he said.

"I'm sorry…I…"

"Don't be sorry. We don't have to do this yet" Malachi said. Tempest sat up.

"You're not mad?" he asked timidly.

"No, it's okay.   Come on...I'll take you home" Malachi said.

Chapter 11

Angel

Malachi sat on his bed in his room. It had been a few hours since he'd taken Tempest back home, and he felt guilty about what had happened. He looked at the picture of them together and spoke his thoughts.

"I shouldn't have made a move. He just wasn't ready. I wish I could help him…I love him" he said. Then Malachi remembered what his grandmother had told him about Tempest being sensitive. He remembered her saying he needed his love.

"I won't push him…I'll let him come to me" he told himself.

Suddenly, his phone rang and Malachi was surprised to hear Tempest on the other end.

"My mom's gone to her friend's house so we can talk in private.   Can you come over?" he asked.

"Uh...sure" Malachi said.

After driving over, Malachi rang the doorbell.   When Tempest answered, his stood in the doorway, holding his stuffed penguin close to him.   Malachi thought this was absolutely adorable.

"Are you okay?" he asked.   Tempest nodded and smiled gently.

"Yeah.   Come in...I want to show you something" he said.

Malachi followed Tempest up to his room. After setting down his penguin, Tempest walked over toward his stereo.

"I want you to hear this" he said.   Malachi watched as Tempest placed a vinyl record single on a small phonograph, and set the needle down to play it.   A melody soon came on, and Malachi recognized it.   It was the song "Angel" by Juice Newton.   Tempest spoke with a calm tone.

"When I play this song, I think of you. According to legend, the name "Malachi" means "angel" he said.   Malachi stood in front of him with tears coming to his eyes.

"Tempest..."

"After looking at our picture, and the

penguin you bought me…I realized you'd never hurt me, Malachi" Tempest said.

"Of course I wouldn't hurt you…not ever" Malachi said.   As the song began to rise in emotion and sound, Tempest spoke again.

"I guess what I'm trying to say is…will you…be my angel?" he asked.   Malachi brought his arms around Tempest and hugged him with great passion.

"I'll always be your angel" he whispered.

As they listened to their song, Tempest felt tears of happiness form in his eyes.   He knew he'd never be alone now, and he then kissed Malachi and they fell upon his bed.   Tempest undid his braid and slowly took off his shirt.

"I'm ready now" he said.

Malachi smiled and began to kiss Tempest's bare chest.   Tempest closed his eyes, and he told Malachi to unzip his jeans again.   Knowing that he was okay now, Malachi took off the rest of Tempest's clothes, revealing his naked body, and then he removed his own.   He got on the bed with him, they allowed each other to feel the warmth of their bodies together, and for the rest of the night…they shared their love.

As the morning sun peaked through the curtains, Tempest laid in the bed next to Malachi. His arms were around him, and he felt secure.

"So that's…love?" he asked.

"Part of it" Malachi said.

"What about the rest of it?"

"It's in our hearts.   The strong feeling you have deep inside you"

"Oh...Malachi?"

"Yeah?"

"I love you...my angel."

"I love you too...my powerful tempest."

Part 2

The Heart of the Storm

Preface

After Tempest Thorn met Malachi Harper, there was a deep connection between the two. Something so remarkable, no human being will ever understand its power completely. It's called love, and it works mysteriously to where it's difficult to predict. Although, now that Tempest has found it, what will he do with the power of love? What also happens when his friends' lives begin to change?

Chapter 12

Rides

It was later in the year now, October to be exact. The bright autumn leaves had already changed colors and most have fallen to the cold ground. Every now and then, the temperature had flocculated and some days would be cooler than others. However, there was no snow. By this time, Tempest and his friends had all graduated from high school. The summer had been nice too. Tempest and Malachi where now able to spend more time together, and with friends. Tempest got a job at the mall in a clothing store, and Malachi liked to come and visit him during his lunch break. Malachi had a job too.   He worked at the ice cream parlor where he and Tempest first met.   It was easy for them to see each other on breaks, since their jobs were both in the same mall.   Also during this time, Frances Fry had published two of her novels. Tempest had always thought she was a talented writer, and he was very proud of his friend. However, he noticed that Frances had quit her job at the bookstore, and whenever he tried to ask her why, she'd simply say she was going to tell him later.

On this day, Malachi realized he and Tempest hadn't been to the nearby amusement park together over the summer.   Since it was nearing the colder weather, he decided to take his boyfriend there while they still had the chance. So, after driving over in his light blue Thunderbird, Malachi and Tempest were now walking around the amusement park.   After being with Malachi for such a long time now, Tempest was more comfortable about being with him in public.   As long as no one bothered them directly.

Malachi sat beside Tempest at a picnic table, playing with his long black braid and drinking pop.   Tempest's hair had gown a little longer and Malachi adored it.
"You're going to mess it up again" Tempest said casually as he licked his vanilla ice cream cone.
"I know, but then I get to re-braid it after words" Malachi said with a chuckle.   Tempest

smiled and gave his boyfriend a small kiss. He knew he loved it when Malachi did his hair for him. In the background, there were sounds of many people in conversations and on the amusement rides.

"We didn't spend too much money today did we?" Tempest asked.

"No, we're fine. Besides, you know money isn't that important to me when we're out together" Malachi said.

"Yeah, but I don't want you to go broke just because of me" Tempest returned. Malachi let go of Tempest's braid and put an arm around his waist.

"You do things for me too. I can't help but spoil you since you're so damn cute" Malachi said softly. Tempest blushed with a smile and got up from the table.

"Let's go on the Ferris Wheel" he said.

"After that, can we go on the roller coasters?" Malachi asked. Tempest cringed for a moment at the thought.

"Um...Malachi, I can't" he said.

"Can't what?"

"Go...on a roller coaster."

Malachi stood up from the table and came close to his boyfriend, putting his arms around him slowly.

"Why not?" he asked quietly.

"I just can't. I don't want...to go through that again" Tempest said nervously.

"What happened before?" Malachi asked. Tempest remained quiet, and he closed his dark blue eyes. "It's okay, you can tell me anything."

"When I was ten, my mom and I came here. She didn't think the rollercoaster would scare me, but…when I went on it…I passed out from fear" Tempest admitted.

"And you've never been on one since then" Malachi added. Tempest nodded. "Its fine, we don't have to go on it."

"You're not mad?"

"Nope; but I'll bet you want to go on the Ferris Wheel, because it's romantic, right?" Malachi lightly teased. Tempest smiled now and nodded again. He knew Malachi could always help him smile and laugh. So, when they rode to the top of the Ferris Wheel, they shared another kiss and enjoyed the view.

Chapter 13

Halloween

Tempest casually put up clothing for display around the store. Many people were at the mall today and he knew most of them were getting ready for Halloween. A new shipment of costumes had just come in, and Tempest's manager, Sandy, told him they all had to be out and ready since Halloween was tomorrow. Tempest thought the place already have enough, but he did his job anyway without questioning. Even though the kids in the store were running around carelessly, as if they're heads had been chopped off, he had to admit, he liked Halloween time.

"You can't touch that" Tempest said sternly, as a little girl pulled down a few displays. The girl simply stuck out her tongue, and ran around the room again. Tempest made a scowl on his face. *"The next time she does that I'm going to rip it out!"* he thought to himself. Then, as if he'd been a knight in shining armor, without the horse, Malachi came in to rescue him from the little demons of the clothing store.

"I thought you *liked* kids?" Malachi asked with a tease.

"I do...just not right now" Tempest said, as he put his arms around his boyfriend. Malachi laughed and kissed Tempest's forehead.

"Since it's almost Halloween, we still have to get costumes" he said.

"What did you have in mind?" Tempest asked.

"Well, I'd be good as a vampire, because I'm the only one who's allowed to bite you. And with you having long black hair and nicely tanned skin, I'll get you a sword with an eye-patch...and you'll make one *sexy* pirate" Malachi said seductively.

"Malachi!" Tempest exclaimed with a laugh.

"What? It's just a nice thought" Malachi said with a smirk.

"Okay, but we're only giving out candy" Tempest said.

"What about after?" Malachi slyly asked.

"We'll see. You have to behave yourself first" Tempest said.

"No fair" Malachi said with a puppy dog face.   Tempest couldn't resist, and as he was about to kiss his boyfriend, the same little girl as before came up behind him and grabbed his long black braid with a hard pull.

"Mr. Ponytail Man?" she asked.

"Ahhh!   What?!" Tempest exclaimed.   The little girl simply looked at him with *innocent* big eyes.

"Do you have anything to eat?" she asked.   Tempest felt like he'd blow his top off.   Malachi chuckled and handed the girl a lollypop from his pocket.

"Here you go" he said.   The girl smiled wide and then stuck out her tongue at Tempest again before running away.   Tempest turned to his boyfriend.

"We're not adopting until we're thirty" he said plainly.

Emma Thorn opened a bag of candy as she got a bowl out of the kitchen cabinet.   It was Halloween night and she knew Malachi would be arriving at any moment.   Meanwhile, Tempest slowly came down the staircase tentatively, wearing the pirate costume his boyfriend had got for him.   He was nervous, because he didn't know what his mother would think.   Emma brought in the bowl of candy and froze when she found Tempest standing by the stairs.

"Oh my...aren't you just the cutest thing!" she said with a smile.   Tempest sighed and straightened his pirate hat.

"Do you think he'll like it?' he asked.

"Honey, he's not going to be able to stay off of you" Emma said with a laugh. Tempest narrowed his only eye not covered by the eyepatch, and blushed brightly.

"Am I supposed to say thanks?" he asked. Emma laughed some more and the doorbell suddenly rang. Knowing it was Malachi, Tempest ran over to the door before his mother could get to it. Nearly stumbling in his boots along the way. Out on the front porch, Malachi stood in his vampire costume. His face had make-up on it, and his hair was all spiked up. He wore solid black and he had his arms folded seriously. Tempest couldn't help but stare with a smile.

"A vampire can't come into someone's home, unless he's invited" Malachi said with a rather terrible Transylvanian accent. Tempest took his boyfriend by the hand and pulled him close.

"You are cordially invited to kiss me" he said. Malachi then cracked a smile and took Tempest in his arms. "So...how do I look?" Tempest asked.

"Perfect, except for one thing" Malachi said. "What?"

Malachi reached behind his boyfriend and undid is long braid. After fluffing out his hair he spoke again.

"Now you're perfect. I like your hair wild sometimes" he said. Emma then walked over to them, holding her purse and car keys.

"I'm going out now, the candy is in the

living room on the coffee table" she said.
"Okay, bye mom" Tempest said.

After Emma left, Tempest and Malachi spent time together watching horror movies and handed out the candy to the trick-or-treaters.   As they lay down on the couch together with the lights off, Malachi noticed a wall full of portraits and other pictures of Tempest and his mother. The lights from the TV barely lit the room, but Malachi could still see them.   He was particularly interested in one photograph off to the far left of the wall.   Behind the plate glass, Tempest stood there holding a baseball bat and wearing a uniform.
"I didn't know you were in baseball before" he said.   Tempest looked up at the picture as well and spoke quietly.
"That was when I was seventeen, shortly before I met you" he said.
"Why'd you quit?" Malachi asked.
"I didn't want to, but...it was the other guys on the team" Tempest said.
"What about them?"
"They...were mean...to other guys like us"
"Oh."
"I was afraid that they might find out...who I really was."
Malachi noticed Tempest was hugging him tightly at the thought of the memory.   He carefully brushed his boyfriend's black bangs from his eyes.
"You know I've always told you that it

doesn't matter what other people think" he said softly.   Tempest felt a few tears forming in his eyes.

"I know, but…it's just so hard sometimes" he said.

"Come on…let's go upstairs" Malachi said.

As they lay together in the bed, with their costumes on the floor, Malachi ran his fingers through Tempest's hair leisurely.   Tempest felt warm and secure when he was with him.   He had told Malachi this many times, since he truly said from the heart.

"I like when you love me like that" he said calmly.   Malachi smiled and kissed him.

"I think you should get back into baseball. You're a fast runner and you're strong too" he said. Tempest closed his eyes, smiling to himself.

"Just be sure to come to my games" he said.

Chapter 14

An Old Acquaintance

Feeling a little tired the next day, Tempest worked at a somewhat slower pace than usual. He yawned off and on while he hung several scarves up for display.   He didn't notice as someone walked up to him slowly.

"I like the red one" said a quiet voice. Tempest looked beside him and was surprised to find Ramona McBee standing there.   She held her purse tightly and looked at him cautiously. Tempest hardly recognized her without her dark make-up on. He sighed and spoke carefully.

"What do you want?" he asked. Ramona let out a nervous sigh and fiddled with her purse's strap.

"I um...came to talk to you" she said. Turning back to his work, Tempest spoke again without looking at her face.

"Where's Nathan?" he asked.

"We...broke up over the summer. I didn't like the way he treated me" Ramona voiced. "How are you and Malachi doing?"

"That's none of your business" Tempest said as he began to walk away.

"Wait! Tempest...I'm...sorry" Ramona blurted out. Tempest stopped and turned to look at her. He was now surprised.

"What do you mean? It's not like *you* to say *sorry*" he said.

"Well...I am. I'm sorry for the way I treated you in high school and...Nathan is an asshole" she said uneasily. Tempest's eyes widened.

"Really?" he asked.

"Yeah. I'm not a mean person...really. I just was lost when I was with Nathan. I would turn into a horrible person and not care about others" Ramona said anxiously. She felt her tears forming and she quickly opened her purse to find a tissue. "I shouldn't even be here...you probably hate me anyway. I'll just leave" she said. Tempest realized Ramona was telling the truth, and he quickly caught her by the wrist.

"I don't hate you...I just didn't like how you

treated me" he said.   Ramona wiped her eyes. She just couldn't seem to stop her tears.

"I know, and that's why I'm sorry" she said.

Malachi suddenly came into the store to greet Tempest.   He soon discovered Ramona standing beside his boyfriend, and he gave a look of extreme protection.   He immediately walked directly over to her.

"What the hell are *you* doing here?" he asked with a dark tone.   Ramona flinched and then spoke.

"You um...must be Malachi" she said.

"Yeah, and I already know who *you* are" he replied with a glare.   He stood directly in front of Tempest, as if to shield him from her.

"Malachi...it's okay" Tempest spoke up. Malachi looked at his boyfriend in bafflement. "She came to apologize to me."

Malachi turned back to Ramona again.

"Is that true?" he asked.   Ramona nodded lightly and wiped her tears again.

"You have every right to be mad" she said. "So...I'm sorry to you too."   Malachi eyes then began to soften.   He moved out of the way, but still stood beside Tempest.

"Are you going to be okay?" Tempest asked.

"Yeah...I'm fine.   Anyway, maybe we could all hang out sometime and talk.   Just to start over" Ramona said.

"Sure" Tempest said with a smile. Ramona stopped her tears and closed her purse.

"Well, I got to go.   I guess I'll see ya later" she said.   Tempest then said bye to her and watched her leave.   He then turned to Malachi.

"Thank you…for staying here" he said. Malachi brushed Tempest's bangs with his hands.

"I'll always be with you" he said with a smile.

Chapter 15

Snowflakes

Tempest noticed that Malachi quite often stayed with him at his house. Not that he was complaining about it, he loved having Malachi with him. However, Tempest couldn't help but wonder if Malachi had something important to tell him. It sort of reminded him about how Frances had been acting. Instead of asking about it, he decided to wait and see if Malachi needed the right moment. He somehow knew it wasn't anything bad, Malachi was just a little nervous.

During that day, Tempest invited Frances to go to the mall with him and Malachi. She had been studying a lot more recently, and she didn't seem to get out much for the past few weeks. Frances didn't complain, she *did* say, however, that she couldn't be out all day, as she had to prepare for things.   Tempest was even more confused by this.   Malachi caught on right away, but also realized that Frances would tell him on her own time.   Another thing Tempest had realized was the fact that Willa and Justin seemed to be spending more time together.   However, they didn't seem to know why.   Tempest knew though, and so did Malachi and Frances.   The three of them had suspected it for quite some time.

While the three of them entered a candle store, Tempest had decided to go and look for a specific scented candle.   Malachi chose this moment to talk with Frances.
"So, when are you going to tell him?" he asked her.   Frances, surprised for a moment, stopped walking and looked at Malachi.   She then remembered how he could sometimes sense things about other people.
"I…don't know" she said quietly.   She picked up a small yellow candle off the shelf beside her labeled *Honeysuckle* and sniffed its aroma.
"I don't want to rush you, but I also know you don't have too much time left…do you?" Malachi asked.   Frances nodded and put the candle back.
"I'm afraid to tell him, Malachi.   His like a kid at heart, and he's so sensitive.   What if…he can't take it?" she asked.
"Give him time.   He's stronger than you

think, Frances" Malachi added.

"Yeah, you're right.   He's probably already realized I've been trying to tell him" she said with a small smile.

"I have something to tell him too.   Or, ask him actually, and I think I'm going to tonight, when we're alone" Malachi said.   Frances knew what it was and put her hand on his shoulder.

"Good luck…I think he'll say yes" she said.

Malachi and Frances then saw Tempest walking over to them with a bag.   Inside, were three scented candles in which he'd bought.   He handed the first one to Frances.

"Here" he said with a smile.   "I know it's your favorite."   Frances was delighted to have been given a hyacinth scented candle, and she hugged her friend.   Tempest then handed Malachi a jasmine scented candle, and he kept a lavender one for himself.   "I thought we could light them tonight" he said with a blush.   Returning a smile, Malachi kissed his boyfriend's forehead and took him by the hand.   He knew Tempest had caught on to him, and wanted them to be alone so they could talk.   In her mind, Frances had given Malachi credit for being braver than she was. Although, she knew she'd tell Tempest when the time was right.

That night, Tempest and Malachi lay in bed together nude, and held each other while their candle's made shadows in the dark room with their flames.   They hadn't engaged in any love making yet, they just simply wanted to hold each other and talk since it was rather cold outside.

"You know, Malachi, we've been together for a long time now. And...*well*...I think I know what it is you want to ask me" Tempest confessed. Malachi, who had been playing with his boyfriend's hair again, suddenly stopped.

"Really?" he asked, and Tempest simply nodded. "Well, if you already know then..."

"No. I *want* you to ask me" Tempest interrupted. Malachi and Tempest looked into each other's eyes while smiling. The glow from the candles magically reflected off them.

"Will you...move in with me, Tempest?" Malachi asked with a whisper. Tempest put a hand on his boyfriend's face gently.

"Yes" he returned. And with that said, Malachi and Tempest kissed and then noticed many white snowflakes floating silently down to the earth outside. Tempest sat up and gazed out the window in awe.

"It's...so beautiful" he said softly.

"Yeah...I think it's snowing...for us" Malachi said. Tempest then felt some warm tears of joy forming. He laid his head down on Malachi's chest.

"I love you" he said.

"I love you too...always" Malachi returned.

Tempest suddenly got an idea. He wanted to do something "new" in his relationship with Malachi. He slowly got out of bed, and opened his desk drawer.

"What are you doing?" Malachi asked. Tempest said nothing. He simply took out something from the drawer and turned back to his boyfriend. In his hands, tossing it playfully back and forth was a container of vanilla frosting. Tempest made a seductive smile, and Malachi gently pulled him back on the bed. "Vanilla *is* my favorite" he said with a smirk.

Chapter 16

Inner Feelings

    The next morning, Tempest woke up underneath his warm heavy blankets.   He felt around with his hands and suddenly realized he was alone.   He quickly sat up in his bed and looked around for his boyfriend with a worried face.   Then, off in the distance in the house, he heard a few noises from the kitchen.   He heard Malachi's voice talking with his mother's and he let out sigh of relief.   He noticed the container of frosting on his desk, with the lid sitting crookedly on the top.   *"I'll never forget that"* he thought to himself with a smile.   He then crawled out of bed and put on some new clothes.   He didn't bother braiding his hair, since he wanted Malachi to do it for him. He just had that *magic* touch.

After coming down the staircase, Tempest's mother came over to her son with a delighted smile.

"Malachi just told me the news, I so happy for you!" she said with tears of glee. Tempest gave a hug and then thanked her for the comment. They walked into the kitchen and Tempest found Malachi at the stove, cooking breakfast.

"You don't always have to make me breakfast" he said calmly.

"Yeah, but nobody cooks for *my* man, but me" Malachi said. Tempest blushed and then sat down at the table with a smile. Tempest could hardly cook anything, and when he had too, the microwave was his best friend.

Later in the day, Tempest invited his friends over to help him pack up his things for the move. Like his mother, they were all equally happy for him. The day suddenly turned tiresome as Tempest realized how much stuff he had. Although, he was glad to have his friends and his mom help him. Malachi did too, of course, and eventually he was going to help him pack his belongings as well. As Willa sat on the floor packing boxes with Frances and Emma, she couldn't help but watch Justin from afar. All day, he'd been carrying many boxes and helping Tempest and Malachi with the heavy stuff. Like he usually did when his body got too hot, he took off his shirt, revealing his muscles and shiny body.

Frances noticed this and she snapped her fingers in front of her friend, waking Willa from her daze.

"What?" Willa questioned.
"You were drooling" Frances said blatantly. Emma giggled to herself, and Willa gave a nervous smile.
"Sorry I...was just thinking" she said.
"Yeah" said Frances. "Are you almost done with the packing tape?" Willa stared at the box on her lap. It didn't have *any* tape on it. She'd been too busy daydreaming over Justin's physique. Willa looked up and smiled again, brushing her red hair from her eyes.
"Almost done!" she said happily. Frances wasn't convinced.

Shortly after packing, the guys, Emma, and Frances carried everything outside, while Willa cleaned up the mess. She realized she'd been thinking a lot about Justin lately. However, she didn't know why. Sure, she thought he was cute, but, she was only his friend, right? Willa sighed and turned around. She suddenly dropped the garbage she'd been holding and stared at Justin standing in front of her. There he was again, shiny as ever, looking right back at her.
"Do you need any help?" he asked.
"Um...I thought you were helping outside?" Willa asked.
"I was...but you were in here by yourself, and..."
"And what?"

"I just thought I'd...help you" he said. Willa was surprised. She found herself looking at every inch of him. *"Honey, you help me with a lot of things"* she thought to herself. She then blushed and shook the thought from her head.

Secretly, Tempest, Malachi and Frances watched them from afar, smiling amongst themselves. Justin walked over to Willa to pick up the garbage on the floor. To his surprise, he was soon stopped by something. He eyes widened as Willa locked him in a romantic kiss. He then wrapped his arms around her in return. For a while now, Justin had been feeling the same way. He just didn't know how to tell her.
"It's about time" Frances said as she walked back in the house. Tempest and Malachi followed behind her. Justin chuckled and Willa simply couldn't stop blushing.

After everything was finally taken out of Tempest's room, Emma came in and found her son standing there, alone.
"Where's Malachi?" she asked him. Tempest turned around quickly, since he hadn't known she was there.
"He's in bathroom. He'll be right out" he said. Emma walked over to the window of the empty room and looked out.
"It's kind of hard to imagine" she said.
"What?" Tempest asked.
"You not being here anymore" Emma said quietly. Tempest saw her tears and he walked

over to her slowly.

"I'll be fine, mom" he said.   Emma turned with a small smile.

"I know.   You and Malachi will take care of each other well.   Just promise me you'll come and visit, okay?" she said.   Tempest then hugged her tightly.

"I will, mom, don't worry" he said.

Chapter 17

Moving In, and Going Away

Tempest and Malachi spent a majority of the time in their new apartment, arranging their belongings into many different places. It was fun, and often out of excitement, they couldn't decide what went where. Later on, Malachi's parents came over, bringing a coconut cream pie. They chatted for a few hours until it was time for them to leave, and Malachi and Tempest finally finished unpacking. They now sat on the couch, a little exhausted.

"Do you think we have too much stuff?" Malachi asked. His arms were around his boyfriend lovingly.

"Nah, all of this stuff defines our personality" Tempest said.   Malachi smiled and gently pushed his boyfriend down on the couch and got on top of him.   Tempest stared up Malachi in surprise.

"Sorry, I just had to ravage ya" Malachi said. Tempest laughed and pulled Malachi down on top of him.

Suddenly, their doorbell rang.   Tempest and Malachi quickly got up off the couch and went over to the door.   After opening it, they found Frances standing there, waiting to be invited in.

"I hope this isn't a bad time, but...I need to tell you something" she said.

"Sure, you can come in" Malachi said. Frances made a small smile.

"Thanks...it's...important" she said softly.

Frances followed her friends into the living room and didn't sit down.

"I can't stay very long" she said.

"What's wrong?" Tempest asked cautiously. Malachi didn't speak.   He knew she had to tell him on her own.   Frances stood there in silence for a moment.   She didn't often get afraid, but she was now.   She looked up at Tempest with saddened eyes.

"I'm..."

"Going away" Tempest finished with a somber tone.   Frances nodded.

"Yeah...to college.   I wish...I'd...told you

sooner" she said in tears.   Tempest felt a melancholy wave come over him.

"You'll be back…right?" he asked sadly.   Frances rushed over to her friend and hugged him.

"Of course I will.   You're my best friend after all" she whispered.   "It's just for a couple of years, and I'll call you every weekend."   Tempest began to sob lightly and he hugged her in return.   They stayed that way…for several minutes.   Frances didn't want to part with him, but…she had to.

"You have a great life now, Malachi will always be here for you" she said.   Tempest pulled back and wiped his tears.

"Okay" he said.   Frances then gave Malachi a hug as well.

"Take good care of him for me" she whispered.

"I will" Malachi reassured.   Frances then walked back out to her car.   Malachi put is arms around Tempest as they watched her drive away down the snowy avenue.

Lying in bed that night, Tempest felt something inside him.   It was a fear of some kind.   He felt as if he was about to lose everyone.   Even Malachi.   He thought about how Willa and Justin were going to be spending more time together now.   It was okay with him, but…something still bothered his mind.   He felt he was going to lose Malachi too, and this thought made him physically shake a little.   Tempest looked beside him at his partner, who was fast asleep.   He put his arms around him, and slowly, he fell asleep too.

Chapter 18

The Bond Between Them

Tempest woke up as the morning sun dimly shown on his face. He nervously felt around the bed for Malachi's presence, but...it wasn't there. Tempest felt the feeling again. It was strong and dominating. Something was wrong...he could feel it deep inside. He vaulted out of bed and quickly got dressed. Outside, Malachi started the engine of his Thunderbird and slowly began to back out of the driveway. On the avenue, a delivery truck was making its way on the icy road, driving faster than normal. Tempest ran over to the apartment door and tried to get it open, but the lock was old and it quite often stuck.

Malachi didn't see the truck.   He backed completely out of the driveway casually.   And that's when Tempest heard it.   A blaring truck horn...followed by a hideous sound of smashing glass and crunching metal.   Tempest's eyes widened and filled with tears.

"No!" he cried.   He slammed open the door with a hard kick, breaking the lock.   He ran as fast as his legs could go.   His tears poured down his face, and his long black hair flowed behind him. *"Please, Malachi...please be okay!"* his thoughts screamed.

He flew out the main door of the apartment building, and down the driveway.   Malachi, meanwhile, had gotten out of his wrecked car, and saw Tempest coming.   He held his arm in severe pain.   Tempest finally saw him too and he dashed into a strong embrace.   He sobbed hard into his boyfriend and wouldn't let go.

"It's okay, Tempest..." Malachi said with his own tears.   "...I'm fine."   Tempest's words were scared and came out crazed and shaky.

"You weren't there!   I woke up and...you weren't there!" he cried.   Malachi put a hand under his boyfriend's chin and brought his head up.   Tempest's saddened dark blue eyes met with Malachi's warm, protective brown ones.

"I'm okay" Malachi whispered.   And with that, Tempest blinked his eyes and took in the reality.   *"He's really...okay."*

Malachi then pressed his lips against Tempest's and they kissed for several minutes.

Tempest waited impatiently in the waiting room of the hospital. He stared down at the floor from where he sat, and was still shaken-up over the car accident. He thought about how he'd gotten the feeling that Malachi was in danger, even before the accident happened. He knew before, that there was a special bond between them. That's what happens when you truly love someone; your inner power can be unleashed.

A doctor came walking down the hall toward Tempest, and Malachi followed. Tempest looked up and saw his boyfriend had his left arm in cast and a sling. During the car accident, the impact made Malachi hit the car door beside him, breaking his arm. Tempest got up quickly and went over to him.
"It was just a simple fracture, Malachi's arm will be fine in six weeks" the doctor said. Tempest then smiled with relief and carefully embraced his boyfriend.
"I don't know what I would do…without you" he said quietly. Malachi smiled back, and kissed Tempest forehead gently.

Malachi got a leave of absence from work, and he stayed home with Tempest and loved him passionately. As they lay together in bed, nude under the blankets, they held each other and listened to music softly echoing in the distance of the bedroom.   Tempest was okay now.   Malachi was back in his arms, and he was okay again.

"I promise you, Tempest…I'll never leave you" Malachi whispered.

"I know…after all…I'm in the arms of an angel" Tempest whispered back.

The two of them fell asleep together that night.   They could rest peacefully knowing they would always be together, no matter what future struggles life had in store for them.   They would get through them knowing neither one of them are no longer alone.   For all they truly needed from then on was each other.   Together, their love is whole and true.

The heart of the storm…is ever powerful.

Author's Notes

This book was very personal for me. I put in some real life experiences of my own into this story, which only certain people would know of. I finished this book about four years after I graduated from high school. I published it originally in 2010, but then again in 2018 with a new publisher. I, myself, "came out" at age seventeen. Many readers have told me that Tempest Thorn resembles me, or at least a side of me. My sensitive side and I would have to agree. I did not write any detailed sexual scenes in this book, because I felt there was no need for it. I've actually been asked about why I didn't write those kind of themes for this story. The romance and love between Tempest and Malachi was shown more in a genial way during their intimate times together.   I didn't want sex being a major theme. Secondly, the characters of this story may or may not make another appearance in my writing, because my life is very different now than what it was when I first wrote this.   This story is like a modern fairy tale romance, and one that hoped for in the past.   I still love this book very much, and it will always have a special place on my shelves...even if life surprised me by going in a completely different direction.   I don't regret any of my experiences with the man I hold close to my heart every day.   I am very blessed to have him in my life.

Printed in Great Britain
by Amazon